The BIG Magic Animal Book

If you enjoy The Big Magic Animal Book,
then you'll love these three huge collections
of fantastic stories:

The Big Book of Dragons
The Little Pet Dragon *by Philippa Gregory*
School for Dragons *by Ann Jungman*
The Bad-Tempered Dragon *by Joan Lennon*

The Big Haunted House Book
Bumps in the Night *by Frank Rodgers*
Spookie Movie *by Claire Ronan*
Scarem's House *by Malcolm Yorke*

The Big Wicked Witch Book
Fisherwitch *by Susan Gates*
Broomstick Services *by Ann Jungman*
The Cleaning Witch *by Cecilia Lenagh*

The Big Magic Animal Book

The Marmalade Pony
LINDA NEWBERY

The Wishing Horse
MALCOLM YORKE

Mr Wellington Boots
ANN RUFFELL

Hippo

Scholastic Children's Books,
Commonwealth House, 1–19 New Oxford Street,
London, WC1A 1NU, UK
a division of Scholastic Ltd
London ~ New York ~ Toronto ~ Sydney ~ Auckland

Published in this edition by Scholastic Ltd, 1998

The Marmalade Pony
First published in the UK by Scholastic Ltd, 1994
Text copyright © Linda Newbery, 1994
Illustrations copyright © Susan Hellard, 1994

The Wishing Horse
First published in the UK by Scholastic Ltd, 1995
Text copyright © Malcolm Yorke, 1995
Illustrations copyright © Jan Lewis, 1995

Mr Wellington Boots
First published in the UK by Scholastic Ltd, 1996
Text copyright © Ann Ruffell, 1996
Illustrations copyright © Jan Lewis, 1996

Cover illustration copyright © Jan Lewis, 1998

ISBN 0 590 54355 5

Typeset by M Rules
Printed by Richard Clays Ltd, Suffolk

2 4 6 8 10 9 7 5 3 1

The rights of the authors and illustrators to be identified
respectively as author and illustrator of their work have
been asserted by them in accordance with the
Copyright, Designs and Patents Act, 1988.

Charlotter
Booklog ✓

Contents

The Marmalade Pony

LINDA NEWBERY

Illustrated by Susan Hellard

To Mariam

Chapter 1

Hannah didn't think she was going to like the new house. It was small, with a little wedge of scrappy garden. All the rooms needed decorating and the bathroom had damp marks on the walls. The road outside was so busy that she wasn't allowed to cross it by herself.

She would have to go to a new school. She felt lonely and missed her friends. There seemed to be no children in their new road. Most of the neighbours were much older than Mum and Dad, with children who had grown up and gone to live somewhere else.

The only person of Hannah's age was a dark-haired girl who sometimes played in the garden next door. Dad said she must be the granddaughter of the man who lived

there. She didn't live there – she only came on Saturdays.

There was no one for Hannah to be friends with.

"You'll make new friends at school," Mum said. "It won't seem so bad in a week or two."

Mum had left her friends behind, too. She was trying very hard to be cheerful. So was Dad. Sometimes you could *hear* them trying to be cheerful, both at once.

"We're lucky I've got my part-time job," Mum said. "Some families are worse off."

Dad just grunted and turned the page of the newspaper. Every Friday, he got up early and went to the newsagent's along the road to buy the local paper. Then he sat down busily at the table with a cup of coffee and a red pen, reading every single job advertisement. By Friday evening, after making lots of phone calls and visits to the Job Centre, he was fed up again. There were so many people looking for jobs.

There was only one good thing about the new house as far as Hannah could see. It was nearer to the country than their old house had been, and there was a riding school along the lane. There were stables and barns, and several ponies grazed in a field where jumps were set up. There were ponies of all colours – black, brown, chestnut, white and a spotty one like a Dalmatian dog. At weekends, and some-times in the evenings, processions of riders made their way past the house, on their way to the woods. Hannah looked enviously out of the window. Some of the riders were about her age.

"Oh, Dad," she burst out. "Could I. . .?"

She stopped, seeing Dad's face. No, of course she couldn't. It would cost too much. But Dad said they'd go down and see. Hannah already wished she hadn't asked, especially when they got to the riding school gate and read the board outside. Lessons £7 per hour, it said. Dad had had to sell the car when he lost his job

at the steelworks, because a car cost too
much to keep. Of course he couldn't afford
£7 for riding lessons. Just once, perhaps,
for a birthday present, but not every week.
To learn to ride properly you had to go
every week.

Dad looked just as disappointed as Hannah.

"I'm sorry, love," he said, as they turned away. "If only it wasn't such an *expensive* hobby."

"It doesn't matter," Hannah said.

They walked along beside the field with the red-and-white poles and barrels in it. Some of the ponies were grazing there, and one of them came up to the fence. It was a small pony, the one Hannah liked best. She had watched them go past the window so often that she knew them all. This one was the colour of caramel, or sticky toffee, or marmalade – the dark kind with thick slices of peel in it. The marmalade pony was usually at the back, jogging along on quick little hooves to keep up with the bigger ponies. It had a bushy mane and forelock the colour of straw, and bright, mischievous eyes. It came up to Hannah and pushed at her hand with its soft nose, as if it knew her.

"This is my favourite," Hannah said.

"I wonder what his name is?" Dad said.

Hannah thought for a minute. "I don't think he's a he," she said. "I think she's a she, and her name ought to be Marmalade."

Dad laughed. "*Marmalade*! I've heard of a marmalade cat, but not a marmalade pony."

"This is one," Hannah said, and she picked some grass for Marmalade, even though there was plenty of grass in the field for the ponies to eat. Marmalade ate it, and Hannah pretended for a moment or two that Marmalade was her own pony. There was nothing to stop her pretending. You don't need money to pretend.

Chapter 2

Dad started behaving very oddly. As well as doing the shopping and cooking, and hunting for a job, he started doing something in the little garden shed. No one was allowed to go in. Once Hannah heard sawing and banging and wondered what he was making. A boat, perhaps? He liked boats. But the sea was miles and miles away.

Perhaps Dad was pretending, too.

Next Saturday morning she found a long list on the kitchen table, in Dad's writing. It said:

Just as Hannah was picturing a glued-together varnished boat, with billowing leather sails tied on with woollen ropes, Dad shouted, "Don't look at that! It's a —"

He snatched the list from her.

"A what?" Hannah said.

"A – a shopping list. Just some things for the house," Dad said, walking quickly out of the kitchen.

Hannah went into the garden, where
Mum was planting tulip bulbs so that the
garden would have some colour in it next
spring.

"What's Dad making in the shed?"
Hannah asked.

"Oh – a something. A – a wardrobe,"
Mum said. "Yes, a wardrobe. That's what
he said it was."

Hannah felt disappointed. The boat
with leather sails would have been more

interesting. All the same, she thought, it must be a very *unusual* wardrobe to need all those ingredients.

For the next few evenings, Dad stayed out of the shed, although Hannah noticed that he smelled of paint. On Wednesday afternoon, he met Hannah at the school gates, looking pleased and excited.

"Have you got a job?" Hannah cried.

"No," Dad said. "But there's a surprise for you at home."

"What is it?"

Dad wouldn't say. He made Hannah wait all the way home. What could it be? she thought. One of her friends from her old school, coming to tea? His new wardrobe? For a wild, ridiculous moment she thought it might be a pony. Perhaps he'd brought Marmalade home. . .

Dad took her into the living room and made her sit down.

"Now shut your eyes and wait for a minute."

Hannah closed her eyes and listened hard. She almost expected to hear the clop of polished hooves on the floor. But there was no sound, and then Dad said eagerly, "You can open them now."

Hannah looked. There was Dad, holding a stick with a wooden pony's head. It was varnished in a colour like toffee or caramel or marmalade, and it had a bushy mane like Marmalade's, made of thick cream-coloured wool. It had little curved ears made of felt. It had painted nostrils and a mouth, and round eyes like buttons. It even had a bridle made from strips of green leather, with big curtain rings for the bit.

"What do you think?" Dad said, full of pride.

"Isn't it lovely?" said Mum, who had followed him in.

Hannah stared. It was only a toy pony –
a hobby-horse. How silly she had been to
think it might have been a real one! But
Mum and Dad were so delighted with it
that she said, "Thanks, Dad. It's great."
And she stroked its mane and pretended
to ride it, holding the green reins and
galloping three times round the garden.
Dad fetched his camera and took some
photos.

"What will you call him?" Mum said.

Hannah thought for a moment. "I don't
think he's a he," she said. "I think she's a
she, and her name's Marmalade."

Dad puffed out his breath with relief. "I
hoped you'd say that."

"Why?" said Hannah.

"Come and see," shouted Dad, and he
raced up the stairs, followed by Hannah,
Marmalade and Mum.

Hannah stopped in her bedroom door-way and stared. "It's a stable for Marmalade!"

"That's right," Dad said, proudly. "Be careful. The paint's not dry."

Dad had cut Hannah's wardrobe door in half so that the top part swung open, like a real stable. Over the top, he had fixed a green plaque, with MARMALADE painted on it in marmalade-coloured letters.

Hannah put Marmalade into her stable. She looked so funny with her head poking out from all the T-shirts and jeans that Hannah laughed.

"I'll be able to lie in bed and look at my own pony in her stable," she said.

Dad looked so pleased that Hannah wished he had a horse and stable of his own.

Chapter 3

That night, Hannah looked at Marmalade for a long time before she went to sleep. Marmalade was only a toy, but in the semi-darkness Hannah could pretend she was real. The street light outside threw Marmalade's shadow against the wall, outlining her pricked ears and tufty mane.

Hannah slept, and then something woke her up, something that sounded like a hoof stamping impatiently. She opened her eyes and looked towards the stable door. She thought she saw Marmalade toss her head, throwing back her thick mane.

"Come on, then," Marmalade said. "What are you waiting for?"

Hannah sat straight up in bed. "You can talk!"

Marmalade snorted. "Yes, of course."

"But you're only a. . ."

"Only a what?" Marmalade said, with a trace of annoyance.

"Only a – well, a toy."

"Hrrrmmpphhh!" Marmalade said, in

the sneezy way ponies have. "In the
daytime, perhaps. Night-time is different.
Now, are you coming or not?"

"But where are we going?"

"For a ride, of course. Now, if you'd
kindly unbolt my stable door. . ."

Hannah got out of bed and slid back the
bolt on Marmalade's door. Funny – she
didn't remember noticing a bolt there
before.

"Thank you," Marmalade said politely
as the door swung open. She clopped out
of the stable, four shiny hooves on

cobblestones. She arched her neck proud-
ly and jingled the bit in her mouth.
Hannah could smell her warm pony smell.
Marmalade pawed at the ground.

"But you're real!" Hannah cried.

"I keep trying to tell you," Marmalade
said.

Hannah blinked several times to get the sleepiness out of her eyes. "I must be dreaming!"

"As you wish," said Marmalade. "Now, are you going to get on, or are we going to stand here all night? It's rather cold for someone as finely bred as myself."

"But how do I get on?" Hannah asked.

Marmalade seemed to think this was too silly a question to bother answering. She just turned her head round and pointed her nose at her back. Hannah saw that she was wearing a saddle, with shiny silver stirrups.

Hannah was still not quite sure. "Can I really. . .?"

Marmalade sneeze-snorted, and Hannah put her left foot in the stirrup and pulled herself up into the saddle.

"A little less of a thump next time, please," Marmalade said, pawing the ground again. "Now, if you'll just put your feet in the stirrups and hold on to the reins —"

"Don't move. I'll fall off," Hannah said in alarm, doing as she was told.

"Of course you won't. We're moving already, hadn't you noticed?"

Hannah stared around her. She thought they had been in her bedroom just a few moments ago, by the wardrobe-stable, but now they were out in the street and the houses were flashing by on each side, making her remember taking off in an aeroplane when they'd gone on a holiday

to Spain. It was just like that now; and even more like it when Hannah saw the ground a long way underneath them, with the street lamps strung out like beads, and the sky above like a big black tent studded with tiny lights. Hannah gave a shriek of

terror which came out as a shriek of delight. Her feet were firmly in the stirrups and her hands gripped the green leather reins and Marmalade's thick mane, and she felt quite safe. She was really riding, and not just riding, but flying!

Marmalade seemed to be in a better mood now that they were airborne.

"Isn't this better than staying in bed?" she called to Hannah.

"Oh, yes!" Hannah gasped as they cleared the dual carriageway. It was like a cross-country course in the sky! Marmalade plunged and dashed and circled and dived. She soared past the steelworks, skimmed over the school, swooped over

the swimming-pool, hovered over the hospital, leaped over the library, plummeted over the playing-fields, banked over the building site and floated over the factories with a flick of her tail. Then she slowed down, falling like a feather towards a row of chimneys which Hannah recognized as her own road.

Hannah's insides felt dizzy and shaken, and she closed her eyes and held tight.

When she opened her eyes again, she was in bed, clutching her pillow. She felt as if she had been asleep for a very long time.

"I must have dreamed it all," she thought. She sat up and looked at the wardrobe stable. Marmalade was there, propped up on her pole. Her button eyes seemed to be looking at Hannah and her painted mouth was curved in the beginning of a smile.

At breakfast, Hannah yawned. Mum said, "What's the matter with you, dozy-head? Aren't you awake yet?"

"I had a tiring night," Hannah said, wondering whether anyone would believe her. "I've been riding Marmalade all night long."

Mum smiled and ruffled Hannah's hair. "You always did have a good imagination," she said.

All day at school, Hannah wondered whether it really was just her imagination. Would Marmalade turn into a real pony *every* night?

Perhaps, if I think about midnight-riding when I go to bed, she thought, it might happen again. But then will it be real, or just a dream?

She thought hard about Marmalade when she got into bed, but she was dreaming about teddy bears and liquorice allsorts when Marmalade clopped over to the bed and nudged her awake.

"Come on," Marmalade said, shaking her mane. "What are you sleeping for? I need exercise. I had to stand in this wardrobe for seven or eight hours while you were at school."

Hannah sat up and rubbed her eyes. "You *are* real!"

"Hrrrrmmph!" Marmalade said in disgust. "How much proof can a person want?"

"I'm sorry," Hannah said. "I —"

"Consider it from my point of view," Marmalade said. "You wouldn't be very pleased if I kept telling *you* you're not real, would you? Now hurry up and get on. I feel energetic. I'll show you I'm real all right.

Hannah put on her dressing-gown, took hold of the green reins and climbed up to the saddle, remembering not to crash down this time.

"Ready," she called

"I hope you are," Marmalade said, with a quick hop on all four feet, like a lamb. "You'd better hold tight. I feel alphabetical tonight. I'm going to arabesque and bascule —"

"What do those words mean?" asked Hannah.

"Hold on and I'll show you," said Marmalade, and she was already in the air, aimed like an arrow, bounding over the railway bridge.

"I'm going to cavort and canter and caper," shouted Marmalade. "I feel like dancing and darting and dodging. I'm going to execute an effortless foxtrot and fandango, I'm going to frisk and flutter, gyrate and gallivant. . ." And she did.

"Gambol and gallop," shouted Hannah, getting the idea. "Hop, hurdle and hoof it—"

"Very funny," said Marmalade, "if we must indulge in inane idiocy. Hold on, I'm going to jig and jive, kick and kink, leap and lurch and – now hold really tight—"

"I am," cried Hannah.

"Loop the loop!"

And she did, an enormous sky-circle, so that the wind rushed through Hannah's hair and the stars were all around her, and she didn't know which way was up.

"That was rather good, if I say so myself," Marmalade said, levelling out over the sports centre. "I feel rather proud. I've never tried that before. Not feeling seasick, I hope?"

"Just a bit," Hannah said, not wanting to stop the aerobatics.

"All right, I'll slow down," Marmalade said. "I'll amble and brake and crawl and dawdle. . ."

But before she could get very far into the alphabet, Hannah was asleep.

Chapter 4

Next morning, Hannah remembered what Marmalade had said about being shut in the wardrobe all day. She carried her downstairs and out into the garden, and propped her up against the garden fence. While she was doing this, she couldn't help seeing that Marmalade was just a toy, made out of painted wood. Marmalade was stiff and lifeless in her hands, and her almost-smile was just a painted line on the wooden head.

The man-next-door's granddaughter was in her garden, wandering about as if she had nothing much to do. When she saw Hannah she said, "Hello," rather shyly, and Hannah said, "Hello," back, and they both looked at each other. Then the other girl ran back indoors. She had a long black glossy plait which bounced on her back as she ran, and she wore silky trousers and a tunic in colours as bright as jewels.

"Her name's Mariam," Dad said, when

Hannah told him that she had spoken to the girl next door. "She spends every Saturday here with her granddad. Her parents run a stall at the market." He had had plenty of time to chat to Mariam's granddad over the garden fence.

"Why don't you ask if she'd like to come in and play with you?" Mum said. "You could show her Marmalade."

Hannah was doubtful. She wasn't sure that Mariam would want to – to say nothing of Marmalade. "I don't know," she said. "Marmalade's a bit tired today. She did a lot of galloping about last night."

She saw Mum and Dad smile at each other. They thought it was just a game she had made up. Hannah looked out of the window at Marmalade and saw a toy hobby-horse sagging against the fence, and wondered for a moment whether they were right.

That night, she went to sleep thinking about Marmalade as usual. Some while later she opened her eyes and saw that Marmalade was still in her wardrobe-stable. The pony looked sad. Her head hung low and her ears drooped.

"What's the matter?" Hannah asked, getting out of bed. "Aren't you coming out?"

"I don't feel in the mood," Marmalade said grumpily.

"But it's the middle of the night," Hannah said, "and we've still got half the alphabet to do!"

"I know," said Marmalade.

"Don't you want to go out at all? Not for a –" Hannah had been practising all day – "a scamper or a skitter, a sidle or a scuttle, not even a single shuffling sidestep?"

"No," said Marmalade sadly. "I feel more like sulking in my stable."

"What's the matter?" Hannah asked. "Are you ill? Shall I fetch a – a vet, or ask Dad to give you a new coat of varnish?"

"No," Marmalade said. "I'm not ill."

"Then what *is* wrong?"

Marmalade looked at Hannah. "I'm lonely. I want a friend."

"Oh, I see," Hannah said.

"Another pony, I mean," Marmalade said. "You're not too bad, but there are some things only another pony can understand."

"Hmm," said Hannah. She stood for a moment thinking. Then she had an idea. "I'll see what I can do tomorrow," she said.

"Thank you. And now, if you don't mind, I'd like to get some sleep," Marmalade said, yawning.

Next day, Hannah took Marmalade out to the garden fence again, and propped her up so that she faced into Mariam's granddad's garden. Two or three times during the day she saw the old man looking at Marmalade, and later she saw him talking to Dad over the fence.

"I think my idea might be working," she told Marmalade that night.

"You're going to find me a friend?" Marmalade said, cheering up.

"Well . . . I hope so."

"This calls for a celebration," Marmalade neighed, undoing the door-bolt with her teeth and trotting out of the wardrobe. "Jump on!"

"Where are we going?" Hannah asked, scrambling up.

"Surprise!" Marmalade shouted. As soon as they were airborne, she set off in a straight line, instead of wheeling and circling as she had done before. Holding tightly, Hannah looked down and saw the silver threads of motorways, the dark huddled woods, clusters of sparkly lights for towns and villages, and once an inky black lake. Ahead, the moon hung in the sky like a big shiny coin.

"Are we going to the moon?" Hannah asked.

Marmalade snorted. "Of course not. I can't fly that far. Wait and see."

Not far ahead, the land was coming to an end. Hannah could smell the saltiness of the sea; below were the sharp cutaway shapes of white cliffs. Waves creamed at the sea's edge, and the moonlight cast a shining rippled track on the sea, leading to the distant place where sea and sky met.

We must have flown for miles and miles, Hannah thought. She shouted to Marmalade, "Are we going to France?"

"*Non!* But hold very tight – we're going down!"

Hannah gripped two handfuls of Marmalade's thick mane and got ready. She thought Marmalade was going to fly down

and land on the beach. Instead, she headed
straight on, out to sea, along the moon's
shimmering path. They were so low over
the waves that salty droplets got into
Hannah's mouth and clung to her hair.
She thought she could see the darting

shapes of fish beneath the water, blue and
grey glints, flashing back the moonlight.
Close by, a dark wave humped itself and
then broke free to leap into the air, a glossy
arching shape in a shower of moon-drops.
A dolphin! Its mouth seemed to be

laughing at them and it joined in their mad gallop out to sea, keeping pace with Marmalade, leaping and diving like a switchback ride, while the fish beneath the surface shimmered like silver fireworks. And then Marmalade was slowing, her hooves sending plumes of spray up from the waves. The dolphin stood up on its tail and back-paddled, and chattered goodbye. Then it dived and was gone.

We've come a very long way, Hannah
thought, miles and miles, far too far to get
back again in one night. . .

But before she had finished thinking,
she was waking up from a long sleep,
yawning and stretching. She looked across

at Marmalade, who was smiling her secret smile again.

"That was a very good celebration," Hannah said. She thought to herself, I hope there really *is* something to celebrate.

When she went downstairs, she let herself out into the garden and tiptoed towards the shed. The door was firmly shut, but she could hear Dad inside, whistling. Through the cobwebby window she could see strips of red leather hanging on a peg. She smiled and crept away.

Chapter 5

That Saturday morning, Hannah saw Dad out in the garden quite early, talking to Mariam's granddad over the fence. Dad came indoors looking very pleased with himself. While he ate his breakfast, he kept looking at his watch. Then he said, "Come outside with me, Hannah. It's time for Mariam's surprise."

"What surprise?" Hannah said, although she had guessed.

"It's her birthday today," Dad said, "and her granddad asked me to make a special present for her."

There was a ring at the doorbell.

"That will be them now," Mum said.

She went to open the front door. Mariam came through to the kitchen, holding her granddad's hand. She looked rather shy because of being in someone else's house, but she smiled at Hannah.

She had brown eyes as lively as a robin's and she wore silky trousers and a tunic of bright turquoise, like a kingfisher. It was decorated with gold and scarlet braid, and she had gold and scarlet ribbons plaited into her hair, to match. Everyone else's clothes suddenly looked very dull.

"Happy birthday," everyone said to Mariam.

Dad led the way out to the garden and then he made Mariam wait with her eyes closed just as he had made Hannah wait. He went into the shed and brought out Mariam's hobby-horse – a pony like Marmalade, a little darker in colour. It had a mane and forelock of pure white wool; it had pricked felt ears and a bridle made of red leather. Its mouth was curved into the beginning of a smile.

Mariam clapped her hands and laughed, and hugged the pony.

"He is a magician, your father," Mariam's granddad said to Hannah.

"I know," Hannah said. She wondered whether Dad knew how *much* of a

magician he was. "I must fetch Marmalade," she said.

"What will Mariam's pony be called?"
Mum said. "Is it a he or a she?"

Mariam looked at her pony and then at
Hannah. "Yours is called Marmalade, isn't
she?" she said. "I think mine is called
Mango Chutney. I shall call him Chutney
for short."

"That's a funny name for a pony," said Mariam's granddad.

"Chutney likes it," said Mariam, cuddling the horse. "Don't you, Chutney?"

Hannah went upstairs to fetch Marmalade. Something was worrying her. She told Marmalade about the new pony. "Will Chutney be a magic pony, like you are?" she asked.

"That depends on Mariam," Marmalade said. "It depends whether she thinks he's a few bits of wood and leather, or whether she thinks he's a pony."

Hannah sighed with relief. "Then it will be all right," she said.

Chapter 6

"You must decide what to wear for the birthday party," Mum said to Hannah when Mariam and her granddad had gone back next door. "It was nice of Mariam to invite you, wasn't it?"

"Mmmm," Dad said. He was busy making a list.

"What are you planning now?" Hannah said.

"Well," Dad said, looking more pleased than ever, "while you were upstairs, Mariam's granddad asked me to make lots more ponies. Mariam's mum and dad run a toy stall at the market. They like to sell handmade things. So I'm going to make

them some. And perhaps –" Dad said, getting carried away, "– perhaps, if they do well, I might think about having a stall of my own! It'd be better than hanging around the Job Centre."

"You and your ideas," Mum said. "Pigs might fly. Still, it's worth a try."

Hannah opened her mouth to say, "Ponies can fly, so why shouldn't pigs?" but then realized how silly it would sound. She caught Dad's eye and he grinned, and then he wrote down something else on his list. She looked over his shoulder. He had written: Pink paint, corkscrews for tails.

Hannah smiled, thinking of a skyful of flying pigs, zooming around like fat pink balloons when you blow them up and then let go without tying up the end.

"Come on," Mum said. "You still haven't decided what to wear. I'll need to iron something."

"Oh yes," Hannah said, thinking of the party. It was a long time since she'd been to a party. Mariam had invited her so that they could ride their ponies together, and groom them, and talk about them. Mariam wanted to be friends. Her plan had worked better than she had expected; they could all be friends now.

Mariam and Hannah.

Marmalade and Chutney.

The Wishing Horse

MALCOLM YORKE

Illustrated by Jan Lewis

Chapter 1

Long ago and far away in another country, there was an old man and a horse. The horse pulled a battered cart which had a notice painted on the side saying:

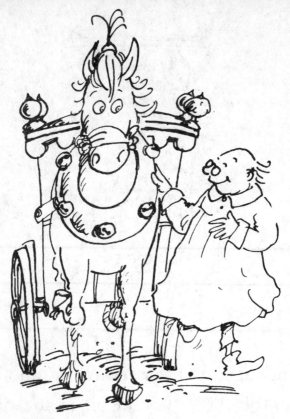

The old man didn't ride in the cart but walked alongside the horse and talked to him.

"I don't think many folk in this miserable place will be able to pay five hundred gold pieces, do you, Albert?"

And Albert said, "Neigh!"

Indeed, the country they were travelling through looked very poor. The roads were full of holes, the cottages were all falling down, the crops were neglected and the cattle looked thin and hungry.

As the old man and Albert were walking along, they met a young man coming towards them. He was dressed in rags and his shoes had many holes in them.

The old man asked him, "Is it far to your main city, young man?"

"About two hours' journey down this road," he replied, "but I wouldn't go there if you can avoid it."

"Why not?" asked the old man.

"Because our selfish king lives there and he's the greediest man on earth. He's just mad about gold. If he sees your old horse and cart he'll make you pay taxes

on them. He taxes everything just so he can live in luxury, counting his gold pieces."

"Oh, dear, he doesn't sound a very nice character," said the old man.

And Albert said, "Neigh."

But they both continued down the road to the big city.

Soon they overtook a bent old woman hobbling along with a stick, and again the old man asked the way.

"Oh, don't go to the city," she said, "you'll get robbed of everything you've got like I did, and all my family."

"Whoever would rob a poor old man like me?" he asked.

"Well, if the king doesn't rob you the queen will. She's so vain and greedy she's robbed us all just to pay for her fancy necklaces and rings and brooches and jewels."

"She doesn't sound very pleasant, does she?" the old man said, as they plodded on.

And Albert said, "Neigh."

A little further on a boy and girl were sitting by the roadside. They were very skinny, poorly dressed and barefoot. When the old man asked them how near the big city was they told him it was just over the next hill.

"But don't go there or you might meet the horrible prince who just stuffs himself with rich food all day long while we go hungry," said the boy.

"Or even worse you might meet the princess who dresses in the most expensive furs and fabrics and has five hundred pairs of shoes while poor people like us don't have even one pair between us," added the girl.

"Well, thank you for warning us," said the old man. "I really don't like the sound of that pair, do you?"

And Albert said, "Neigh."

Nevertheless, he and Albert still kept moving steadily in the direction of the big city.

Chapter 2

Pretty soon, they were over the hill and could see the city before them. The people's houses were overcrowded and falling down. The windows were broken, the doors hung off their hinges and tiles were missing from the roofs so the rain could get in. As they walked through the streets the old man and Albert saw many beggars, but nobody seemed to give them anything because the people were nearly as poor as beggars themselves. In some places they saw lines of prisoners shuffling along with chains on their necks and ankles – they were the poor people who couldn't pay the king's cruel taxes.

"I don't like this place one little bit, do you, Albert?" said the old man.

And Albert said, "Neigh."

When the old man asked directions to where the king lived, people looked frightened and warned him not to go there, but eventually he and Albert arrived at the main square and on the far side of it they saw an enormous palace.

There was a high wall round the palace with guards marching along the top, but they could still see that inside the walls there were blossoming trees and gold-covered turrets and pinnacles.

They went up to the iron gates and the old man knocked.

"I'd like to meet the royal family, please," he said.

"Meet that awful lot! Whatever for?" asked the guard, looking very surprised.

The old man pointed to the notice on the side of his cart:

"I want to sell them some magic wishes," he said.

"It's us poor people who need magic wishes, not this greedy royal family," exclaimed the guard. "They've got everything anybody could wish for anyway – enough food, warmth, clothes, money, a palace – everything."

"Maybe," said the old man, "but I've never met anyone yet who didn't wish for more, no matter how much they had."

"Oh, they'll wish for more all right because this is the greediest family that ever lived," said the guard.

"And don't forget my price is five hundred gold pieces," said the old man, "and from what I've seen none of the ordinary people here could afford that."

And Albert said, "Neigh."

"It still doesn't seem fair to me," said the guard, but he let them in and sent a messenger ahead to ask if the royal family would like to see this seller of magic wishes. The old man and Albert were led through beautiful gardens full of flowers and statues and fountains, where strutting peacocks were the only living creatures enjoying them. Eventually, they were shown through

the gold doors of an enormous hall, richly furnished, thickly carpeted and hung with crystal chandeliers which twinkled in the firelight. At the far end, on a platform, were four thrones.

On the biggest one sat the king. He was fat and sweating in his long robes and his heavy crown. He was counting gold pieces into a chest which was on the table

at his side. The queen was even fatter and was dressed in an awful purple dress and shoes, both covered in jewels. She had a gold crown, too, and three rings on every finger. By her side sat the prince, busily scoffing a whole fruit cake from one hand, and scooping up handfuls of strawberries and ice-cream and stuffing them in his mouth with the other hand.

The princess was trying on fifty pairs of shoes, one after the other, and throwing the ones she didn't like into the fire. All in all, the royal family was not a pretty sight.

Chapter 3

"Now," snapped the king, "what's this nonsense about magic wishes? Speak up and be quick about it."

The old man pointed to the sign on his cart:

ALBERT
THE
MAGIC HORSE
WISHES GRANTED
500 GOLD PIECES
EACH
EVERY ONE A WINNER

"Every one a winner?" said the king suspiciously.

"Indeed, your majesty. You see, my magic horse Albert here" (Albert nodded his head to the king) "grants wishes. You can have as many as you like until you are satisfied, but each one costs you five hundred gold pieces."

"It's a lot of money, so this had better work!" snarled the king, as he handed over five hundred gold pieces from the chest which stood near his throne. "Now I wish for lots of gold!"

The old man nodded, went over to Albert and whispered in his ear.

And Albert said, "Neigh."

There was a sudden flash of lightning in the room and. . .

The king was frozen solid in the middle of
a gigantic ice-cube!

"Quick! Quick!" shrieked the queen, and the servants came running with hammers and axes to break up the ice and buckets and kettles of hot water to melt it. Eventually the king staggered out looking absolutely furious, but his teeth were chattering so hard he couldn't speak. He just stood dripping in front of the fire, plucking icicles out of his whiskers.

"I'm awfully sorry about that, your majesty," said the old man. "Albert's getting a bit deaf and he must have thought you said lots of COLD."

"My turn now!" said the queen, and
with her plump jewelled fingers she
counted out five hundred gold pieces
from the chest. "I know I am very
beautiful already, but even so my wish is
for great glamour."

Again the old man whispered in
Albert's ear.

And Albert said, "Neigh."

There was a flash of lightning and. . .

Out of the air appeared a colossal
mallet which bashed the queen over the
head and flattened her. The servants

rushed to help her to her feet and to straighten all the bent prongs on her crown. The queen was very angry indeed, but she had such a splitting headache she couldn't speak.

"Oh, tut-tut, Albert, you really must listen more carefully! I do apologize for him, your highness – he must have thought you said GREAT HAMMER."

"I'm next," said the prince, putting down a half-eaten pork pie and digging into the chest of gold pieces with his sticky hands. "And what I wish for is lots more food; for example what I fancy right now is an enormous jelly."

The old man whispered in the horse's
ear.

And Albert said, "Neigh."

The flash of lightning came and. . .

The prince became fatter, and fatter, and fatter, blowing up until he was as round as a football. All his buttons went pop! and his trousers split up the seams. He rolled off his throne and bounced down the steps and across the hall. The servants caught the bouncing prince and wedged him in a corner where he very slowly deflated. He was extremely peeved, but all he could utter was a little squeak, like air coming out of a balloon.

"Now Albert, that really was too bad. I clearly said an enormous jelly, not an ENORMOUS BELLY. Now please do concentrate. I can only say I am extremely sorry, your majesties," said the old man.

"Me! Me! Me!" shrieked the princess, who had now finished with the shoes and had begun to try hats on in the mirror beside her throne. She looked in the mirror again and said, "Obviously I'm pretty, but now I wish to be very *very* pretty."

As before, the old man whispered to
Albert.

And Albert said, "Neigh."

The lightning flashed and. . .

. . . nothing seemed to change – most
certainly the princess did not become
prettier. Instead she began to scratch.

She threw away her crown and had a good tear at her hair. Then she tore off her jewels and shoes and dress and underclothes and scratched and scritched away at every limb. She jumped up and down and howled as the servants sprayed her with flea powder and dunked her head in a bucket of water. She really was hopping mad, but the flea powder had got up her nose and all she could do was sneeze and sneeze.

"Oh, deary, deary me, Albert, how ever could you mistake pretty for NITTY? He really can do better than this, your majesties, I promise you. Now, would anybody like to try again?"

Angry as they all were, the royal family could see that Albert really did have magic powers, so they all had another turn. And, of course, they paid five hundred gold pieces for each wish.

This time the king wished for great power and was instantly soaked by a GREAT SHOWER which poured cold water on him. He had only just got

warm after his ice-cube experience and now his teeth were chattering again.

The queen tried once more and this time she wished for a lot of money. She immediately found herself covered in HONEY and it took a long time to chase all the angry bees away. The

servants had to scrape the sticky mess off her with spoons.

The royal family were extremely cross by this time.

Chapter 4

"Your magic horse has messed up every wish we've made," shouted the king. "Now you've one last chance before I send you both off to prison!"

"I really can't understand it, your majesties. Things don't usually go wrong when people make their magic wishes, do they, Albert?" said the old man.

And Albert said, "Neigh."

Now the prince and princess were both greedy, but they weren't stupid. They had a think and a whisper together and then the prince said to the old man: "I can see there's some real magic at work here, but it keeps going wrong every time we wish for something for ourselves. This time I want to try my wish out on somebody else first and see what happens to them."

"What a good idea, your majesty," said the old man, as he took yet another five hundred gold pieces from the prince.

"Follow me," said the prince, and he led the king, queen, princess, the old man and Albert out on to the balcony which overlooked the city. From there they could see the main square where the poor people were going about their miserable lives.

"See that poor thin man shopping in the market there? The one followed by all his hungry children?" asked the prince. "Right, my wish is that they could enjoy a feast fit for a prince."

The old man smiled and whispered in Albert's ear, and Albert said, "Yea."

There was a flash of lightning and. . .

The poor man was suddenly loaded with shopping bags full of fruits and vegetables and meats and cheeses and jams and cakes. All his children found their arms full of wonderful things to eat and drink. They were astonished

and set off laughing for home to cook a feast for all their family and friends.

"Now, that time my wish did come true," said the prince, "and didn't those poor people look happy!"

"Now it's my turn again," said the princess. "You see that beggar woman dressed in rags by the palace gates? My wish is that she is clothed as finely and warmly as a princess."

Well, the old man smiled and whispered in Albert's ear.

And Albert said, "Yea."

There was a flash of lightning and. . .

The beggar woman was instantly
dressed in warm, bright, clean clothes
with fine boots and even a hat with a
curly feather in it. She looked down at

herself in amazement, then went dancing joyfully across the square to show everyone how her fortune had miraculously changed.

"That was fun," said the princess. "I'd never realized how nice it is to help people like that."

Chapter 5

The king and queen began to get the idea now. The queen said, "You see that tumble-down dressmaker's house across the square? The one with holes in the roof and broken windows? I wish that it could be made into a beautiful dwelling fit for a queen."

And it was. The roof sprouted lovely red tiles, the windows had glass and

curtains, the paintwork shone and a
beautiful garden sprang up all around it.
The dressmaker came out of her new
front door looking astonished, and then
invited people inside to look at her
wonderful new house.

"I enjoyed that," said the queen, "and wouldn't it be marvellous if everybody had a house like that!"

Next, the king said, "I wish those wretched prisoners tramping past the palace gates could lose their chains and be free."

And they were. They looked at their bare wrists and ankles in surprise, then

laughed and danced all round the square with glee. A lot more people joined in, and soon there was a large crowd cheering and dancing in the square below the balcony.

"Well," said the king, "that wish made a lot of people feel better, including me."

Then the four royal personages went to one side and had a little discussion.

"Have you noticed," asked the princess, "that if you wish for something just for yourself the wish goes wrong?"

"And if you wish for something good for somebody else," observed the prince, "then the wish is granted."

"And wasn't it nice to see all those folk being happy instead of miserable for a change?" said the queen.

"Yes, it was," agreed the king. "Let's ask the old man if we can wish for more good things for the poor."

Then they returned to the old man and Albert.

"Could I wish that ALL our people had warm, clean clothes to wear?" asked the princess.

"Could I wish that ALL the people had enough to eat?" asked the prince.

"Could I wish that ALL the people could earn enough money to live on?" asked the queen.

And the king asked the old man, "Could I wish that everybody in our country could learn to like us?"

"Well, yes," said the old man. "Of course you can wish for all these things, if you really want them."

"We do, we do, we do, we do," they said.

"But unfortunately Albert cannot grant them," said the old man.

"Oh no! Why not?" asked the king in dismay.

"Look," said the old man. "Your chest has no gold pieces left in it to buy any more wishes."

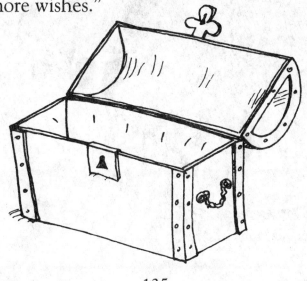

And Albert said, "Neigh."

"I'll sell all my jewels to buy some more wishes," said the queen.

"I'll go on a diet and use the money I save to buy more wishes," said the prince.

"And I'll sell all my silly fancy clothes," said the princess.

"Yes, you should certainly do all these things, but I'm afraid poor Albert has no more magic left in him at the moment."

And Albert shook his head and said, "Neigh."

"Then what are we to do to help all our people?" asked the king in despair.

"Well, if you think about it, your majesty," said the old man, "you can grant every one of those wishes yourself without using any magic at all."

And he and Albert left the room, and the palace.

When it was dark, the old man went round the town putting gold pieces through the letter-boxes until they were all shared out. Then he and Albert

travelled on to the next place where people needed to learn how to use their wishes properly.

As they left the country, the old man said, "I don't think the people here will be cold and ragged and hungry any more, do you, Albert?"

And Albert said, "Neigh."

Mr Wellington Boots

ANN RUFFELL

Illustrated by Jan Lewis

For Selina and her friends

1. The White Elephant Stall

Chapter 1

Mr Wellington Boots was a witch's cat, only nobody knew. Selina, her mum and dad and her brother Peter had found Mr Wellington Boots outside one day. He was yowling very noisily.

"Oh, poor little thing!" said Selina's mum. She picked up the cat and brushed off the dust from its fur.

The poor little thing smiled a sneaky cat-smile, and thought it might stay if the food was all right.

"Isn't he lovely?" said Selina. "Can we keep him? I'll call him Mr Wellington Boots."

"Whatever for?" said Peter.

"Because he's got them on," said Selina.

That was why they didn't know he was a witch's cat. Instead of being all black, he was only black up to his knees. The rest of him was a nice, smoky grey.

"Bring him inside," said Mum. "We'll get him a saucer of milk and ask around to see if anyone owns him."

But of course nobody came to say they owned him. His witch had gone off for a long holiday to a Very Black Forest and left him to look after himself.

Mr Wellington Boots smiled his sneaky cat-smile and slurped up all the milk. Then he put on a hungry look and tipped his head on one side.

"Give him some of the liver we've got for tea," said Selina. She hated liver.

Mr Wellington Boots smiled another sneaky cat-smile. The old witch had only given him old fish heads to eat. So he moved in and lived royally on real tinned cat food and the occasional lump of teatime liver.

Soon after this there was going to be a Garden Fête in the school grounds.

Selina had never been to a Garden Fête before.

"It's a sort of market with stalls," said Mum. "Only it's better because you know the people on the stalls."

"It's a sort of party with lots of things to do," said Dad. "Only it's better because you don't have to do them if you don't want to."

"It's a waste of a good Saturday," said Peter. "And a waste of good pocket money."

"But I'm going to help Mum on one of the stalls," said Selina. "It's the White Elephant stall."

Selina had never seen a white elephant before. She'd only seen an ordinary grey elephant once, at the zoo.

"Why don't you want to help on the White Elephant stall?" she asked Peter. Peter was going to help Dad with the clock golf instead. "You're not scared of white elephants, are you?"

Peter laughed very noisily. "Don't you know?" he said. "White Elephant stalls don't sell white elephants!"

"What do they sell, then, Mister Clever?" said Selina.

"Old rubbish!" giggled Peter.

Selina knew he was quite wrong, but she asked her mum, just to make sure.

"That's right," said Mum. "A White Elephant stall is full of things people don't want. Like white elephants."

"Why don't people want white elephants?" demanded Selina. "I'd like a white elephant."

"Out in the wild, they'd stand out against

the grey ones," said Mum. "The rest of the herd don't want them because they get noticed and hunters might come along and shoot them all."

"That's true," said Dad, "but I know a different story. In India white elephants are very special. In fact, they're so special that people used to give them away as presents. But you need a lot of room for an elephant, and they're expensive to keep. They're not like cats."

Mr Wellington Boots gave a satisfied purr.

Dad finished his story. "So though you were supposed to be grateful, most people didn't want to be given a white elephant for a present."

"I wouldn't mind if someone gave me one," said Selina.

Mr Wellington Boots began thinking, but he said nothing.

Chapter 2

On Saturday Selina woke up early. She couldn't wait for things to start happening.

"Why are mornings so long when you're waiting for something to happen?" she asked Mr Wellington Boots. "I do wish Peter hadn't told me there aren't any real white elephants on a White Elephant stall. I was looking forward to them."

Wellington Boots golloped away at tinned tuna . He thought he might as well do a bit of cat-witchery, just to cheer Selina up.

At last it was time to go and set up Dad's clock golf and get the White Elephant stall ready. The Garden Fête was going to open at two o'clock, and there was a lot to do before then.

There were lots of mums and dads and teachers on the school field. They unpacked boxes and cases and carried heaps of stuff across the grass. Nobody saw the grey and black cat crawling under a stall.

Mrs Speed next door came up to Selina. She was carrying a box.

"Something for you, Selina. You're on the White Elephant stall, aren't you?"

"Yes," said Selina, and held out her arms for the box. She nearly didn't bother to look inside because she was sure it was going to be something very boring. Something nobody wanted. Only there was a funny, snuffly sort of sound, and the box moved in her arms.

Mr Wellington Boots gave a cat laugh under the stall.

Selina peeped inside the box.

It was a very small, very baby white elephant, about as big as a piglet, with blue eyes and very shiny toenails.

Mum turned round and jumped when she saw it. "You can't put that animal on my stall," she said.

"Why not? It's a white elephant," said Selina.

"I suppose it is," said Mum. "All right. Only don't let it be a nuisance. I'd better get some straw from Daddy's clock golf."

Dad had edged his game with bales of straw to stop the golf balls rolling too far.

"I thought elephants ate buns," said Selina.

"Hay, and leaves and vegetables," said Mum. "Only it will have to make do with straw because that's all we've got. Keep it away from the Garden stall. I don't want us to get into trouble because it's eaten all the tomato plants!"

Several other people came to Selina's stall with their white elephants. She knew then that Peter and Mum and Dad had been quite wrong. A White Elephant stall was exactly what it said it was.

"Oh, my goodness," said Mum when she came back with a bag of straw. "I think we're going to need a bit more straw than this. What are we going to do with them all?"

"Sell them," said Selina.

"But nobody wants white elephants," said Mum.

"I do," said Selina, and stroked the very small, very baby elephant with the blue eyes and the very shiny toenails.

Chapter 3

Selina's White Elephant stall became very crowded. There were tall ones, small ones and middle-sized ones. All of them were white except for one very old one that was a bit grey about the ears.

It had been brought by Mr Attfield across the road, and it began to cause trouble right away. It didn't want to stand tidily with the other elephants. It had been boss in the far off place where it had once lived, and it wasn't going to stop being boss now.

It lifted up its trunk and let out a terrific scream.

Selina and her mum and Mr Attfield and everyone else nearby put their hands over their ears.

"Naughty elephant," scolded Selina when it had finished. "Just behave yourself."

Mr Attfield's elephant put its trunk down. Nobody had ever spoken to it like that before.

It lifted its trunk again to give another scream, but Selina told it off again. "I'm ashamed of you," she said. "You're the oldest elephant here. You should set an example. Stop behaving like a baby."

Mr Attfield's elephant hung its head. Its grey ears began to glow red. Old bossy elephants don't usually get scolded by small girls.

It turned its head and walked away so that nobody should see it. Unfortunately it walked behind the Smash-a-plate stall.

Selina's friend Hannah was arranging the old plates on a shelf. It was a lovely stall. You got three balls for your money, then you could throw them as hard as you liked and smash as many plates as you liked.

The old white elephant didn't know this. It poked its trunk through the canvas at the back. Hannah screamed, and ran to tell her dad.

Hannah's dad began to run. He was too late. Mr Attfield's elephant had knocked down four shelves full of old plates. It had knocked down the four shelves as well.

"We're not even open yet!" shouted Hannah.

"I'm very sorry," said Selina. "Can I help you put the shelves back?"

"I'll do it," said Hannah's dad. "Just you keep that elephant away from here."

By now the other elephants were getting out of hand. It was all Dad's fault, really.

This is what happened.

The White Elephant stall was right next to the Hoopla stall. Peter's best friend Tim was busy hanging hooks in difficult places. If you threw all your hoops on to hooks you got a prize.

Selina's dad had finished setting up his clock golf. He came over to see if everyone else's games were working properly. He aimed a hoop at one of the hoopla hooks.

Selina's dad shouted, "Got it!"

And he had. But it wasn't a hoopla hook. It was the trunk of a middle-sized elephant called Hooky, which had been standing very well behaved and minding its own business.

But even well-behaved elephants get startled when someone throws a hoopla hoop over their trunks.

Hooky galloped off in panic. As he went he knocked over a pile of coconuts waiting to be put on to stands for the coconut-shy.

The coconuts rolled all over the place.
Children jumped over them as they rolled.
Mums and dads carrying things didn't see
them. They rolled over the rolling coconuts
and dropped their pot plants, hockey sticks
and boxes of cakes. Another lot of mums and
dads fell over the pot plants and hockey sticks.
Some of the children thought it was a good
idea to try out the cakes.

167

Mr Wellington Boots opened his eyes under the White Elephant stall. He smiled a sneaky cat-smile. Everything was happening just as he had planned.

Then he saw Selina. She was the only person trying to catch Hooky.

Mr Wellington Boots sneezed. Hooky waved his trunk, wondering why he was there, then turned round and came back to Selina's stall.

"Phew! We're all ready now," said Selina. "It's nearly two o'clock."

Mr Wellington Boots smiled another sneaky cat-smile and went back to sleep.

Chapter 4

Selina made Hooky stand at the back of the stall. The elephants were all in rows so that they could be seen properly.

At two o'clock Mrs Pope, the head-mistress, opened the Garden Fête. Selina had to keep her elephants quiet. It would be awful if they ruined Mrs Pope's speech by trumpeting too loudly.

After the speech everyone came to buy
things from the stalls and Selina's proper job
started.

"How much, Selina?" asked Mrs Pope,
patting Hooky on the trunk.

Selina looked at the label Mum had stuck
on him. "Fifty pence, please," she said.

Mrs Pope handed Selina the money.

Then a very strange thing happened. As Mrs Pope walked away with her elephant on a string, the animal seemed to shrink. Its ears, instead of hanging down like mud flaps, stuck upwards and grew points. Its feet stuck together and the toenails turned into round, wooden wheels.

It wasn't an elephant any more. It was a wooden horse with its tail missing.

Underneath the stall, Mr Wellington Boots yawned a wide, pink yawn, and smiled his sneaky cat-smile. He curled up in the other direction and went back to sleep.

"Just the thing for the school nursery," said Mrs Pope, delighted.

Then more people came queuing up to buy a white elephant.

And the odd thing was, each elephant turned into something that person really wanted – a lampshade, or a basket of hair-slides, a half-full bottle of scent, or a jigsaw with only two pieces missing.

At the end of the Garden Fête, there was only one white elephant left.

It was the one Mrs Speed had brought, the first one on the stall. The one that was just the size of a piglet, with blue eyes and shiny toenails.

Selina turned to Mum who was counting the money they had taken on their stall.

"I haven't spent any of my pocket money," she said. "Do you think. . .?"

Mum looked at the small white elephant with the shiny toenails. It had behaved beautifully all day.

"Are you sure?" said Mum.

"Quite sure," said Selina. She tied a string round the small elephant's neck and said, "Come on, it's time to go home."

The small white elephant lifted its trunk and gave a funny, snuffly kind of sound. Under the stall Mr Wellington Boots woke up properly and decided it was time he went home too.

When Selina led the little white elephant away everybody watched. But it didn't turn into a vase, or a pair of matching book-ends, or even a set of coat-hangers. It stayed a very small white elephant with blue eyes and very shiny toenails.

Mr Wellington Boots smiled a very sneaky cat-smile and jumped on to the elephant's back. He wasn't going to walk home if he could help it.

2. The Zoo Thief

Chapter 1

Selina's elephant grew. He still had blue eyes and shiny toenails, but he was not small any more. She called him Hank, because he was as big and white as one of Dad's hankies.

Now he was too big to keep at home.

"Don't worry," said Dad. "We'll ask the zoo to look after him. I'll help you write a letter."

A few days later a reply came from the zoo.
This is what it said:

Appledown Zoo

Dear Selina,

We would be very pleased to look after your
white elephant. We have no elephants of this
colour in our zoo. We will arrange collection
next Monday.

Yours sincerely,

J. Hackett, Director.

On Monday a very large horsebox arrived outside Selina's house. "It's our special elephant transporter," said the driver.

"You could get ten of our elephant in that," said Dad, and called Selina to bring Hank out from the shed.

"He's not very big," said the driver.

"He's too big for our house," said Dad.

"I can see that," said the driver. "But he'll rattle about in there."

Hank could smell delicious new hay at the back of the elephant transporter. He ran up the ramp with no trouble at all.

Mr Wellington Boots wondered what all the fuss was about, and slipped inside the elephant transporter too. The driver didn't see the cat go inside. He barred the door.

"Can I go with him?" asked Selina.

"Sure. Hop in," said the driver.

So Dad and Selina hopped in the front.

At the zoo Dad and Selina hopped out. So did Mr Wellington Boots. Nobody saw him because he slid straight under the booth which says PAY HERE.

The keepers came to meet Hank.

"We've never had a white one before," said one of them.

Selina had to ask the keepers a question. "Will Hank be quite safe? Will the rest of the herd try to get rid of him because he's white?"

The elephant keeper was quite sure they wouldn't. "He would only be dangerous to them in the wild," he explained. "They're all safe here in the zoo."

Selina met the other elephants. They sniffed at Hank, and Hank sniffed back. Then they went off together to find some hay.

The elephant house was warm and cosy, and they had a big field to walk about in. There were plenty of people to look at, and there was plenty of hay to eat and plenty of straw to sleep on.

Mr Wellington Boots explored the zoo. He thought it was cold and draughty. Hay and straw were prickly. He preferred Mum's chair or Selina's bed. And the food didn't look so good. He went back to the PAY HERE booth to wait for Selina.

"I think Hank will be very happy here," said Selina, "but I'm going to miss him like anything."

"You can come and help whenever you like," said the keeper. "We always need people to clean the cages and feed the animals."

Mr Wellington Boots listened from under the PAY HERE booth. He thought he might as well come to the zoo with Selina a few times. He wasn't going to clean cages and feed animals, but he might find some fish to eat in the penguin pool.

They had to take the bus home from the zoo.

Mr Wellington Boots came out from the PAY HERE booth just in time.

"Look!" said Dad. "There's a cat just like Mr Wellington Boots!"

"It *is* Mr Wellington Boots," said Selina. "How did you get here, Boots?"

Mr Wellington Boots tried to tell her, but nobody listened. The zoo keeper found a cardboard box to put him in.

"You can't have a cat running wild in a bus," said the keeper.

Mr Wellington Boots tried to tell everyone that you *could* have cats running wild in a bus, but nobody listened. They tied the box up with string.

He ran round and round the box in the bus, just to prove you could have cats running wild in a bus. Dad and Selina were very glad he was inside the box.

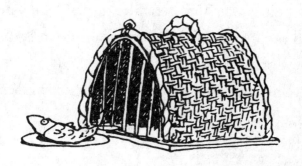

Chapter 2

Selina went to the zoo every Saturday and Sunday to look after Hank and to tell him that she hadn't forgotten him. Hank was happy with his new friends in the zoo, but he was even happier when Selina came to visit him.

Dad bought a special basket for Mr Wellington Boots to travel in when they went on the bus. He grew very fat on fish.

One day there was a new keeper in the children's zoo. He was cleaning out the chinchilla rabbits' cage.

Selina was surprised. She thought she knew all the keepers in the zoo. This one must be a new one.

She was just going to go up and say "Hello", when she saw a strange thing. The new keeper suddenly picked up a chinchilla rabbit and stuffed it under his coat.

No wonder she didn't know this keeper. He wasn't a keeper at all. He was stealing the rabbits!

Selina thought she knew why. People make fur coats out of chinchilla rabbit fur. If he sold them, he would get a lot of money.

There was nobody about. Most of the real keepers had gone off for their tea. All the visitors had gone to watch the sea lions being fed.

She had to do something by herself.

Mr Wellington Boots was very full of the penguins' fish. He curled himself round her legs.

"Good old Boots," she whispered. "You'll help, won't you?"

Mr Wellington Boots smiled a sneaky cat-smile. He might help, if it wasn't too much work.

"You'll trip him up if he tries to get away, won't you?" she whispered, walking over to Hank's paddock.

The white elephant winked one blue eye.

He would help Selina too.

Selina began to rake Hank's paddock. With each stroke she got closer and closer to the children's zoo. Hank followed her.

The thief turned round and saw her. Selina pretended to be raking very hard.

Out of the corner of her eye she saw him tuck another rabbit under his coat. He must have very big pockets, she thought.

Suddenly the thief moved. He was walking away from the children's zoo.

"Come on, Boots!" yelled Selina.

She ran to the thief and tried to grab him by the coat. He was too strong for her and pulled himself away. Mr Wellington Boots didn't want to be trodden on. He thought of a better idea than tripping up the thief.

Selina shouted for the keeper over by the sea-lions' lake. She shouted for the other keepers who were having their tea. But they were all a long way away. By the time they got to her the thief would have escaped with the rabbits.

But Hank the white elephant was ready for him. He coiled his long trunk round the thief's leg and pulled him over.

Then something very strange happened.

Six large dead fish fell out of the thief's pockets. They were very old fish. The smell was horrible! The thief held his nose, and

three more fish fell out of his sleeves. They were very old too. The smell was disgusting!

The keeper could smell them as he ran from the sea-lions' lake.

The rest of the keepers smelled them. It spoiled their tea. They came out to find out what the stink was.

"He's stolen the chinchillas!" explained Selina.

The zoo thief couldn't believe he had his pockets full of smelly fish. He had to think fast. "I thought the fish were spare," he said. "I took them for my cat. I don't know anything about chinchillas. Look."

He pulled out several smelly fish tails from his left boot, and four fish heads from his right boot.

"Oh, Boots," said Selina. "I think we've made a mistake."

"Pooh!" said the keepers. "What a stink! Pick up those revolting things and put them in the bin," they shouted. One of the keepers picked up the brush they used for cleaning cages. "You'll have to clean up the smell," he said.

Mr Wellington Boots yawned – a wide, pink yawn.

The zoo thief thought he had got away with it. But when he picked up the penguins' fish bucket he yelled and dropped it. It was full of furry, squirmy, chinchilla rabbits.

"So you don't know anything about chinchillas, eh?" said the keepers.

The zoo thief tipped the chinchillas out of the bucket.

"Don't let them escape!" shouted Selina. "We'll never catch them if they burrow into the ground."

The zoo thief thought *he* would escape now that everyone was running about after the rabbits. But Hank put a very large foot on top of his coat to stop him from running away.

Lots of zoo visitors came to see what all the noise was about. They helped to catch the rabbits. Selina caught five chinchillas and put them back in their cages. The elephant keeper caught another seven. But it was

Hank who caught the last one. He kept his
foot on the thief's coat, so that he didn't get
away, then with his long trunk he picked up
the last chinchilla rabbit and gave it to one of
the keepers.

Another of the keepers ran to phone the police, and the thief was taken away. He still smelled of rotten fish.

"Well done, Hank," said the keepers.

Mr Wellington Boots thought he ought to have been thanked as well, but nobody listened to him.

The director of the zoo was very pleased. "I'm glad you asked us to have Hank," he said. He invited them to a special tea the next day so that he and his keepers could say thank you properly.

Dad and Mum and Peter and Mr Wellington Boots were invited too. Peter said it would be hay and raw meat, but it wasn't. Hank had extra hay, but the children had sandwiches and cake and ice-cream and all the things they liked best.

Mr Wellington Boots was given a whole pail full of fish, all to himself.

It was a funny thing, but he didn't feel very keen on fish after catching the zoo thief.

3. Mr Wellington Boots' Holiday

Chapter 1

It was holiday time again and the family was trying to find Mr Wellington Boots.

Mr Wellington Boots hated being left behind. He knew he would like playing on the beach just as much as Selina. He didn't see why he should go to the cattery. Ordinary cats went to catteries, but not a magic cat like him.

So he hid behind the bushes in the garden, but Selina knew where to look for him there. When Mr Wellington Boots heard her coming he ran and hid in the shed by the rakes and hoes. Peter knew where to look for him there so he ran and hid in the cupboard under the stairs. Dad knew where to look for him there so he ran and hid in the garage, under the car. Mum knew where to look for him there so he ran into his cat basket. No one thought of looking for him there.

The family had rented a cottage, right by the sea. They collected their spades and buckets and fishing nets and packed them into the boot of the car. Mum remembered the sleeping bags. Peter remembered the cases. Dad remembered the picnic basket, at the last minute.

"But where is that cat?" shouted Dad. "How can I take him to the cattery if he isn't here?"

"Why can't he come with us?" asked Selina. "He's a very good cat."

"You can't take cats to the seaside, stupid," said Peter.

"Mr Wellington Boots is different," said Selina.

Mum and Dad agreed that he was a different cat, but that didn't help find him.

"Can he come if we do find him?" asked Selina.

"Of course not," said Dad. "I've booked him in at the cattery."

But they still couldn't find Mr Wellington Boots. Mum gave Mrs Speed a key and asked if she would feed the cat while they were away. Dad had to ring the cattery to cancel Mr Wellington Boots' holiday. Selina went to the zoo to say goodbye to Hank. She promised to bring the keepers some seaside rock.

When they were all ready to go, Mr Wellington Boots climbed out of his cat basket and into the picnic basket. Nobody

saw him. Dad put the picnic basket in the back seat of the car with Selina and Peter. It was a tight squeeze.

Not far down the road a funny noise came from the engine.

"Oh, no, not already!" said Dad. He stopped the car and raised the bonnet to have a look.

Mr Wellington Boots smiled a sneaky cat-smile in the picnic basket.

"I think I've found the trouble," said Dad. He brought out three bottles of milk from under the bonnet. "Who put them there?" he said, glaring at Peter.

"Not me," said Peter.

"Not me," said Selina.

"It must have been someone," said Dad. "We don't need that much milk."

He put the bottles in the back seat with Selina, Peter and the picnic basket. It was a very tight squeeze.

Dad drove on. A little bit further down the road another funny noise came from the engine.

"Oh, no, not again," said Dad.

He stopped the car and Mum opened the bonnet to have a look. Inside were six tins of cat food.

"Selina, you knew we couldn't bring Mr Wellington Boots," said Mum. "We can drink up the milk but nobody wants cat-food sandwiches."

"But it wasn't me," said Selina.

"Nor me," said Peter.

Mum put the tins on the back seat with Selina, Peter, the picnic basket and the three bottles of milk. It was a very, very tight squeeze.

Further on it was time to stop for their picnic.

"There, Dad!" shouted Selina. "That's a good place."

"Too late, I've gone past it now," said Dad, and drove on.

Ten minutes later Peter shouted, "There, Dad!"

"There's somebody right on my tail. I can't stop now," said Dad, and drove on.

Suddenly there was a funny noise from the engine.

Dad stopped in a hurry, and four cars hooted behind him. "I suppose we'll find the cat basket wrapped round the engine now," said Dad crossly.

Peter lifted the bonnet. "There's nothing here except the engine," he said.

Dad looked as well. Peter was right. There was only an engine.

"What a lovely place for a picnic," said Mum. It was the best of all. They had stopped by a wood, with a space to park the car and plenty of places to walk.

The children ran into the trees and found a grassy glade to have their picnic.

Dad brought out the picnic basket, and they spread out the rug on the grass.

"I'm looking forward to this," said Dad.

He opened the basket. There was no picnic inside, only Mr Wellington Boots, purring gently.

Dad was not pleased. "Where's my picnic?"

he asked. "How can I drive all the way to the seaside without food? And whose idea was this?"

"Not mine," said Peter.

"Not mine," said Selina.

But she was pleased. Mr Wellington Boots would have to come on holiday with them after all. It was too far to take him back home, and Dad had cancelled the cattery.

Mum looked in the boot. One of the sleeping bags had come unrolled.

"What a funny place to pack a picnic," said Mum. She took out the boxes of sandwiches, the apples and bananas, and several bags of prawn cocktail crisps from the unrolled sleeping bag.

"*You* packed the sleeping bags," said Dad. He was still cross.

But Mr Wellington Boots didn't care. He ate some cat food and drank some milk. Then he went to sleep in the picnic basket.

Chapter 2

Mum and Dad did not enjoy their holiday. It rained on the first day. It rained on the second day. The sun shone on the third day and they went down to the beach. Dad's nose got sunburnt. On the fourth day Mum's back got sunburnt. Mr Wellington Boots decided he didn't like sand. It got into his fur.

But Peter and Selina went down to the

beach every day and swam in the sea. They were enjoying their holiday.

On the last day Dad's nose had turned brown and Mum's back had stopped feeling sore. Dad woke up early and woke Mum. "It looks nice. Let's go for a trip on the ferry," he said. "We'll take the camera and a picnic."

The ferry went across the bay from the harbour to Cliff Tops.

Mum yawned and tried to go back to sleep, but Dad wanted to have a good end to this holiday.

Mum made them all eat breakfast and make sandwiches before they went out.

"Don't roll the sandwiches in a sleeping bag this time!" joked Dad.

"It wasn't me," said Mum.

"Nor me," said Selina.

"Nor me," said Peter.

"Then it must have been the cat, because it wasn't me," laughed Dad.

"Has somebody fed him?" asked Mum. "We'd better shut him in the cottage. We don't want him to run away on our last day."

So they shut Mr Wellington Boots in the cottage and went down to the harbour to catch the ferry to Cliff Tops.

Mr Wellington Boots didn't think being shut in a holiday cottage was a good place for him to spend his holiday. He found a window open in the bathroom and jumped out. He followed the family down to the beach, making sure they didn't see him.

The harbour was full of fishing boats and seagulls.

"Look, there's a catamaran," said Peter. It was a boat with two hulls, like two canoes stuck together. "We should have brought Boots after all. It's just the boat for him."

Mr Wellington Boots sniffed at the catamaran. He thought it was a very boring boat. The fishing boats smelled much better. A seagull zoomed down like a fighting aeroplane and chased him off.

"Look – there's a cat just like Boots," said Selina.

"It can't be," said Peter. "We've shut him in the cottage."

"Anyway, Boots wouldn't let a seagull chase him away," said Selina.

They watched the ferry come in, so they didn't see Mr Wellington Boots smile his sneaky cat-smile. But they did see a whole lot of model aeroplanes suddenly fly round the fishing boat aerials, chasing the seagulls away.

"There must be a model aeroplane club here," said Dad.

"I can't see anybody working them," said Peter. He looked round, but it was time to board the ferry.

It wasn't a big ferry. There was only room for about twenty people. There was a cabin where the engine was, but the people had to sit out in the open on wooden seats. Above the engine cabin was a tall mast with a flag on top.

"No cats," said the ferry man. He could see Mr Wellington Boots waiting to get on.

"Of course not," said Dad. He thought Mr Wellington Boots was safely locked inside the holiday cottage.

The ferry man was having a bit of trouble with the model aeroplanes. They kept flying round his engine cabin so that he couldn't see to steer the boat out of the harbour.

Mr Wellington Boots jumped on to the ferry while everyone was bothered about the model aeroplanes. He hid under a seat.

"Drat these models!" shouted the ferry man. He grumbled to the boy who helped him collect the fares, "How do they expect me to do my job?"

Dad went up to the front of the boat and tried to see who was operating the models. Peter went to the back and tried to see from there.

Selina suddenly saw Mr Wellington Boots under a seat. She sat on the seat and put down a hand to tickle him under the chin.

"How did you get out, Boots?" she whispered.

Mr Wellington Boots yawned a wide, pink yawn, and the model aeroplanes flew away. The seagulls came back, but Mr Wellington Boots was under the seat and they couldn't see him.

"Funny," said Dad. "I couldn't see who was working them."

The ferry man glared at Dad as if it was all his fault. He pulled a knob in the engine and the ferry boat made a noise like a lorry. It churned up a lot of oily water, and began to move out of the harbour.

The seagulls shrieked and squawked round the boat.

"This is nice," said Mum. She put on her sunglasses.

"Wait a minute," said Dad. "We're going the wrong way."

The ferry was going out to sea, and not to Cliff Tops at all. They had caught the wrong boat. It was going to the island several miles away. It was a much longer trip and would be more expensive.

The boy who helped the ferry man came round to collect the fares. Dad felt in his pockets. He hoped he had enough money. "Did you bring your handbag?" he asked Mum.

"Did you remember your pocket money?"
he asked Peter and Selina.

None of them had.
Dad counted his money.
"Just as well I've got enough," he grumbled.

Chapter 3

There were big waves outside the bay. Water began to splash over one side of the boat.

Some of the passengers put up umbrellas.

"I can see you've made this trip before," said Dad to them.

Selina and Peter were getting wet.

"Come over to this side," said Mum. She moved so that they could both get in. But Mr

Wellington Boots was still on the splashy side of the boat, and he just hated water!

"Let me take a photo," said Peter. He focused the camera at the waves and at the people with their umbrellas. But there was something else in the viewfinder. "It's Boots!" he cried.

"Don't be silly," said Dad. "We've locked the cat in the cottage."

"It looks just like Boots," said Mum.

"It can't be. It must be the ship's cat," said Dad. He settled down to watch the island come nearer.

Poor Mr Wellington Boots was getting wetter and wetter. He crawled out from the seat on the splashy side of the boat, but the deck was covered in sea water. The ferry man steered the boat right into an enormous wave. Water flew up over the engine cabin. The passengers with umbrellas moved them just in time to catch the water. Mr

Wellington Boots didn't see the wave coming, but the wave saw him. He felt the water slop right into his face. It was like being hit with a hundred wet fish all at the same time.

The cat streaked right up to the top of the flag mast. He clung there, holding on to the flag by his claws, and yowled.

"Help!" shouted Selina. "That's my cat!"

"That's why I said No Cats," shouted the ferry man. "Bring it down before it rips my flag to shreds."

"We've got to rescue him!" cried Selina.

More waves splashed into the boat. The passengers began to panic.

"Help! There's too much water in this boat!" shouted one of the passengers. She pushed her umbrella at the waves to try and stop them coming in.

"We're sinking!" yelled another passenger. He took his swimming trunks out of his bag, ready to swim for it.

The boy who collected the money called the lifeboat over the radio. "SOS! We're drowning!"

Then Mr Wellington Boots gave an immense yowl and a huge fish like a small whale flopped into the boat. It opened its mouth and all the people shrieked. The big

fish sucked in the water that was sloshing
about in the boat. It sucked in one of the
umbrellas too. Then Mr Wellington Boots
hissed and the big fish slurped out of the boat
again.

"I thought we were done for then!" said Dad.

"Save my cat!" shouted Selina. "Hang on tight, Boots!"

Peter took a photograph of Mr Wellington Boots hanging on tight, high up on the flag mast. Selina tried to climb the mast to rescue him.

"Get down!" said Dad.

"What can we do?" cried Mum.

But there was another boat, coming nearer and nearer. It was the lifeboat.

"Help!" cried Selina. "Please rescue my cat!"

"Cat?" said the lifeboatmen. "We came to rescue *you* from drowning, not a cat."

"We're okay – a big fish came and sucked all the water up," said Peter, but the lifeboatmen didn't believe him. When the ferry man told them the same story they said he must have been out in the sun too long.

"Please rescue my cat," said Selina. "He's frightened."

The smallest lifeboatman climbed up the mast to rescue Mr Wellington Boots. Boots put out all his claws to scratch him.

"Don't scratch, Boots. He's coming to help you."

Mr Wellington Boots wasn't too sure about that. But he only gave the lifeboatman a very small scratch, just to show him who was boss.

"Thank you very much!" said Selina. She cuddled a very wet Mr Wellington Boots.

"Don't mention it," said the lifeboatmen. "But don't bring cats out to sea again."

"I *said* No Cats," said the ferry man.

The lifeboatmen sailed away to rescue someone else. The children waved, and Mr Wellington Boots waved too.

Chapter 4

At last the boat stopped at the island and all the people got off. Peter carried the camera and took pictures of the island. Selina cuddled Mr Wellington Boots.

Dad picked up the picnic basket but he tripped on the gang plank and suddenly he didn't have the picnic basket any more. He fished it out of the sea with the end of somebody's umbrella, but it was too late. The apples and bananas were all right, but the sandwiches were very soggy.

"I don't like salty wet sandwiches," said Peter.

Mr Wellington Boots decided he wouldn't help this time. He had had enough of magic for one day. He yawned, showing his pink mouth and his spiky teeth. Then he went to sleep in Selina's arms and refused to wake up.

Dad found a café. "This is becoming an expensive day," he grumbled.

They had to wait in the rain for the ferry to go back again. It was too expensive to stay in the café all the time. Selina tucked Mr Wellington Boots inside her jumper, but he got wet all the same.

And Dad had to pay for the cat to travel on the boat. Both ways.

They arrived back at the cottage. Mum turned on the fire and Dad made some tea.

"Next time we come on holiday that animal is going to the cattery," said Dad. "I don't care how long it takes to find him."

Mr Wellington Boots didn't argue. This was the last time he would take his family on holiday!

"It will be nice to be home," said Selina.

The family agreed with her. Mum looked forward to weeding the garden. Peter and Dad looked forward to watching a football match on TV. Selina looked forward to the zoo, and going to help with Hank.

But Mr Wellington Boots didn't look forward to anything. He was warm and full of food already. He didn't mind where he was, so long as it stayed that way!

The End